As I Sit with Who I've Become

Jakob Ramirez

Contents

Alone and in the Dark............2

Entering the Light...............20

MLM...........................38

Pain and Heartbreak...........58

Putting the Pieces Back
Together..........................78

What Lies Ahead...............101

1

Alone and in the Dark

Before I knew

Kids would always ask

"Are you gay?"

To them, NO I would say.

But what did that mean?

Was it something that could be seen?

My sexuality was a topic

For everyone except me.

The thoughts were so loud

The confusion was so tense

I could not allow the attraction

Since my ego was playing defense.

For a long time I suppressed it

I just hoped that maybe one day

It would all just go away.

I lived in constant turmoil

My mind telling me to ignore

what I felt in my heart.

It felt like I was drowning

The overthinking was unbearable

The sadness was consuming.

Living with a secret

An inner struggle so to speak.

Is it wrong to admit

That I was ashamed?

That I was disgusted?

That I was to blame?

The Truth Will Set You Free

Anxiety ran through my body

Keeping me in a hyper vigilant state.

I was fearful of my desires

I was even full of self hate.

I hid from the world

Putting on a fake persona.

With every chance that I got

I tried not to get caught.

But what was I running from?

None other than the truth?

"Pray the gay away"

I thought that something was wrong

That with me God made a mistake.

I would pray every night

In hopes that God would get it right.

It took me a while to realize

That they would not answer

That I would not change.

Lost and abandoned

Like the world had given up on me.

Hopeless and scared

That my secret would escape.

I had to put up walls

Finding a drive to survive.

High school was all a disguise.

Being a teenager was difficult

Especially one who was gay.

Each of those 4 years were filled

With everything but acceptance.

I carried my secret with me

Like a textbook in my backpack

That would never get opened.

I hid my reality from the other kids

Always finding ways to create new

illusions, anything that would prevent

the truth from escaping.

Every encounter felt like a test

To see if I would give it away.

Having girlfriends left me feeling empty

Showing affection only made me cringe

Kissing her lips when I felt nothing, or

Holding hands and wanting to run away

Further supplied the transparency

Of any possibility that maybe I was

Just pretending to be straight.

Self hatred and internalized homophobia

Robbed me of my chance at teenage love.

Resentment has chased me down every time

Im reminded of what it is that I lost.

To partake in an encounter of naive, young love

And made blind of what it really is

Will never be a part of my teenage stories.

Witnessing media depictions and narratives

Of the kind of love that I missed out on

Forever haunts the teenager that lives inside me.

Some people will never understand

What its like hating yourself

Or what its like being hated

For what you cant change.

Anytime I was around the other boys

I felt sick with apprehension.

My mind would forcibly switch itself

To being in a state of high alert.

Awareness of my sexual validity

Created a victim of vulnerability.

The magnitude of fearing that they

Would eventually figure it out or

That I would somehow be questioned

Left me stranded in a sea of numbness

Where I couldn't figure out how to flee.

Talking about crushes

Being asked about girls

Always finding an excuse

To draw attention away.

She didn't exist because

It was a him, not a her

Infatuated with guys

He captured my heart.

<u>Teenage Love</u>

Seeing other boys being intimate with the girls

Only led me to ponder in jealousy and sorrow.

I longed for the company of a boy

But shame stole my willingness to allow it.

I dreamed of holding hands with him

Receiving endless amounts of kisses

And pressing our bodies up against one another.

A gay version of teenage love that

Would unfortunately never come true.

All I wanted was to be understood

Despite not being capable of it myself.

If only there was somebody to sit with

Reassuring me that I wasn't alone.

Should they feel what I had felt then

Maybe the burden wouldn't have been so heavy.

How do you navigate years of repression

Immobilized by the fear of others opinions

Fueled through the critiques of self hatred

Secluded from a lack of faith in any of the

Possibilities that might linger and await?

If only he could see

Thats who he's meant to be.

Everything would be alright

Even when he came to see the light.

He would become a man

That would learn to give permission

To the feelings inside

Allowing them to no longer hide.

Entering the Light

An Old Friend

You brought on my sexual awakening

Enabling me to finally understand

Yet with that came the downside

To what was simply unattainable.

Falling for you when I shouldn't have

Resulted in my delusion that there

Could be something between us.

Two realities on opposite spectrums

An actuality to what I wanted to believe.

My perception and admiration of you

Would always remain on a one way street.

A failed expectation of you feeling the same

Grounded in hope that we could be more

Instead of just the friends that we were.

<u>Acceptance</u>

It felt like I was a burden

My existence a mistake.

Every day was a battle

A competition to see

If I would break.

I wanted to scream

I wanted to hide, perhaps

I even wanted to die.

All I knew, was that it was true,

and there was nothing that

I could attempt to even do.

Choosing to be free

Free to love whomever

Wasn't just for me

But for him as well.

His dreams are mine

Inside he still resides

With patience and hope

That they'll be fulfilled.

Experiencing your love

Relights his existence

Giving meaning to a voice

One that was never heard.

My First Encounter

Devising a plan to meet up with him

Whilst being behind everybody's back

Brought excitement to my curiosity.

The night finally came where I snuck away

Making the hour drive to see this guy

Who was nothing more than a stranger.

Not knowing what to expect or to feel

The only thing I could do is think as

Fear and guilt battled against my quench

For the freedom to be with who I wanted.

After that night, I was the never the same

Becoming free from doubt in who I was

With certainty in the direction I was headed.

A College Party, Freshman Year

There you were standing with your friends

I remember looking over, wondering about you.

I was mesmerized by the strength of my attraction

That I noticed I began to feel for you.

At the time, I wasn't out yet, but for some reason

I didn't even seem to care.

The fraudulent life that I was living

Left me feeling depleted

Yet in that moment of our fateful encounter

The voice inside my head convinced me to do it

Leaving that night to be the last night

Where I would live my life as straight.

A Secret No More

The sun grew brighter

The sky became wider

I could finally breathe.

A vast space began to open,

For which I could find hope in.

A new place, a new feeling

I was finally beyond the horizon.

When I first came out, I identified as Bi. It wasn't that I was, but it just seemed easier. The Bi label allowed me to dabble in a world of Homosexuality while still serving the Heterosexual expectation that I felt was demanded from me. It was a compromise between the fear of rejection and the feelings of relief. If I didn't say that I was gay, then I wouldn't be forced to deal with the fact that I was still coming to terms with my own acceptance.

At first it felt like a crime

But I knew I had to give it time.

It took some getting used to

But by then I had realized

The life that I had always dreamed of

Was now sitting right in front of me.

Who are they to judge?

To question my rights?

Denounce my existence?

And turn who I wish to love

into what they deem

A political debate?

Do you have any idea how hard it was for me to come out to my dad? He would be the last obstacle in my path to confronting the clash between my old life and the new one I was adamant on living.

Coming out is Constant

You think it would be a relief until life goes on, new encounters and friendships are formed, and then you're teleported back in time to the same person that you were when you first let people in. Its a never ending process whose terms and conditions were never even mentioned, although somehow expected of you to just know.

Hearing the words

"Oh I already knew"

Or "I had a feeling"

Completely destroyed

Any of the faith

That I had within

Of my capabilities

To hide it so well.

It is an absolute blow

To the constant effort

That it took to

Convince the others

That I was not.

Phrases like those

Only contributed to

All my overthinking

That I must've done

Something to give it away.

Finding yourself again is scary

The scariest part of growing up

Is losing your innocence after

Having forced yourself to hide

From the toxicity of masculinity

By concealing your sexuality.

Alternatively you've abandoned

Your truth of who you really are

Up till it finds its way back

Pressuring you to confront an

Internal world that has sat

Untouched and deserted

For what feels like forever.

There is beauty in being gay

Staying true to yourself

Not wanting it any other way.

Affirmations

I am gay

I am strong

I am beautiful

I belong.

I am me

I am free

I am complete.

MLM

Kissing girls

I felt nothing.

Kissing boys

I felt everything.

You make me want to sit in silence

Just admiring all thats in front of me.

No words are necessary

Your presence is enough.

Driving in the car

With my hand on your lap

I glance over

At any chance I get.

To see your beautiful profile

Your eyes facing forward

A smile on your face

I cant help but grin.

How did I get so lucky?

How did I end up here?

My heart skips a beat

Every time I see you cheese.

I am in awe of your beauty

The way you blush

The way you smile.

All I ask, is that you stay

For more than just a "while."

The First Time

The sensual feelings of allowing

Myself the experience of a man

Annihilated every ounce of previous

Curiosity that once lingered within.

Pleasure simply blinded me as the

Union of our bodies took place.

A rush of adrenaline and euphoria

Spread through me from head to toe

Where suddenly shamed ceased to exist

As my desires became more profound.

He slides his hand across my cheek

Pulls my head a little closer

His lips meet mine, and

We lose track of time.

My heart begins to race at what

Feels like a million miles an hour.

My face feels flush, I cant help but blush.

From Boys to Men

I look at us and ponder

That the men we've become

Were once two little boys

With an absent understanding

Of our same sex attractions.

Despite the difficulties it brought

Somehow we've managed

Finding the courage to love

In a world of so much hate.

Each second that we spend together

The more I fall in love with you.

Every minute that we spend apart

The more I wish to be in your arms.

Boy #3

I lay in bed

And I think about your touch.

The smell around your neck

And the taste of your lips.

I wish to see your pretty face

And hear you call my name.

Your presence echoes across my mind.

Being on the lookout for an excuse

To steal all the cuddles

That I repeatedly seek from you.

Your contact serves as a blanket

Doubles as protection too.

You give me no trouble

When I make it known

I just want your affection.

Wrapped around you like

Theres strings attached

Physical touch is definitely

My love language unmatched.

The way your body starts to tense

While your facial expressions

Begin to display excitement

Further propels all of my interest

In exploring the domains of your temple.

Watching you squirm when my hands caress you

As I tease your sense of satisfaction

Brings me much pleasure and gratification

Making it all more worthwhile in hearing you

Call out for my intimacy.

Grateful for your love

The compassion it entails

Patience it exudes

And lack of contingency

Even if it means

Experiencing it only briefly.

Mourning and Grieving

The lights are off

Your head is on my chest

The covers are pulled over us

Underneath our legs intertwined.

You close your eyes

Preparing to fall asleep

Mine stay open as I cant help

But stay awake and think.

While laying with you in bed

I mourn the night time ending

And grieve the mornings arrival

For I know you will have to go.

Although in practice we will see

Each other again, it feels like our

Time together is always short.

When we are apart, your absence

Feels like forever and my body

Feels deprived of your touch.

Gay love is beautiful. I admire it so much. The resilience that men pose when society wishes to keep us trapped in between the parallels of Patriarchy, Masculinity, and Heteronormativity. They label our existence with slurs such as Fag or Queer, however we still remain, including the love itself. Existing centuries before us, its longevity continued through those who refused to deny themselves a chance, at an opportunity of romance.

Love is a double edged sword

While it pays to be this much in love

Pain serves as part of the cost

Stuck in a never-ending nightmare

With no where to run except back to you.

My inclination becomes attachment

In sufferable in every possible way

As the depths of my love for you

Grow at a painstaking rate.

Not ashamed to proclaim my sexuality

But in all honesty, it sometimes feels

Unfortunate that my love is reserved

For other men, most being undeserved.

I hate it here

Top or bottom?

How big is it?

Do you host?

Want to come over?

Hook up culture defines us

Sex is idolized as everything

Relationships are meaningless

Questions like these form the basis

For dating in the 21st century.

Although I yearn to be loved

Attention that I receive is

Instead, a form of lust where

Im viewed as an object

Subjected to their sexualization.

Yet who am I to complain when

In reality I too do the same

Viewing men as nothing more

Than a means of pleasure.

Falling victim to the ludicrous

Broken cycle of emotional instability

That raves amongst our community

Of men loving men.

Pain and Heartbreak

Our first and only valentines

I bought and made him a basket.

What did I get?

A sorry ass explanation

Where he said he had planned

On buying me flowers

But chose to buy alcohol instead.

The Boy I Met at a College Party, Freshman Year (Pt.1)

I knew something was off

When everything started to add up.

The way he would tilt his phone

While texting, only when I was nearby.

The unanswered phone calls and text

messages where it seemed like I

was being purposely ignored.

The excuses that never made any sense.

And when I asked for access to his phone,

the anger and defensiveness that he displayed.

The Boy I Met at a College Party, Freshman Year (Pt.2)

At first I thought it was just my insecurity

Until my internal alarm continued to sound

Louder and louder forcing me to pay attention.

My instinct told me that he was

Yet I willingly chose to dismiss it.

When the opportunity arose for his

Unfaithfulness to be exposed

I begged him for another chance

Hoping he wouldn't leave me.

It should've been the other way around.

My first love

My first sexual partner

My first heartbreak

My first betrayal

My first glimpse

At what could go wrong.

<u>Boy #3 (Pt.2)</u>

I watched you slip away slowly

As I began to notice all the small signs.

The hearts that you would text me

Were no longer part of our conversations.

Your effort and consistency

Became half assed and sporadic.

My heart understood what was happening

So I knew I had to ask you about it.

You reassured me that everything was fine

Little did I know, we were running out of time.

My feelings continued to grow for you

While yours seemed to stretch paper thin.

Suddenly the world went dark

And happiness couldn't be found.

Pain and exhaustion filled the tears

That would run down my face

Every day that I was reminded

That you were no longer here.

I felt trapped, stuck in between

A wall of hurt and confusion.

The thought of you coming back

Was just my own delusion.

Your absence had a profound

Impact on me and my mental state

Because in losing you I lost myself too.

Cant you just pick up your phone

Send me a text

Tell me that you miss me?

An action that seems so simple

And really doesn't take a lot.

You may think that I'm desperate

Or still so attached,

But I just want to know

That this wasn't all for nothing

That I did mean something to you.

Something New

Isn't it crazy,

That when something new happens

Who do I think of, but you?

Since then my life has unfolded

Theres so much I wish to share.

If only I could update you,

Yet you probably wouldn't even care.

My phone chimes

I hope that its you.

Sadly its not

But what can I do?

I cant help but wonder

Do you think about me too?

I am a prisoner of your love

Your mere existence so to speak

Forever etched into the walls of my heart.

It seems like I cant get rid of you

Though you were able to get rid of me.

They say I have to let you go

Yet deep down I know I dont want to.

I dont want to give up

Even though you clearly have.

I dont want to accept

That there is no longer a "we"

Or that our time together is finished.

I guess I'm just afraid that

You and I were only a fantasy.

A moment in time

A glimpse at love

Until you walked away.

No Contact

Im tired of thinking about the what ifs

I would just like some answers

Perhaps closure to be exact.

Give me one last talk, and

Let us close out this chapter.

I am not sorry for loving you

I am not sorry for giving you my time

I am only sorry that we didn't make it out

together.

I love

I love you.

I loved

I loved you.

Maybe it was my own delusion

Maybe I let myself get too attached

Or maybe I was in the wrong place

Searching for love, that with you,

Didn't exist.

Hopefully your love for him

Is stronger than it was for me.

Most importantly, hold on to him

Like you couldn't do with me.

Texts from his phone

"Thank you for loving me the way that you did.

Because of you, I was able to come out to my

family."

As I sat there,

Tears running down my face

I kept reading those words,

And it became clear to me

My love was truly rare.

Maybe in another universe

Another timeline

Our love is still operating in union.

Maybe we are still laughing

Maybe we are still smiling.

Putting the Pieces Back Together

I thought I was in love with you

But really it was only the idea of you.

Passing through your city

All I hear is your name

All I see is your face.

Things once so insignificant

Now all too extraordinary.

You might've left

But the memories have stayed.

Me and You

A story of

Twin Flames

Forever stuck

On two

Different planes.

<u>Love must be forgotten</u>

When I look up at the sky

And see the moon,

I still think of you.

When I stand on the shore

And the waves crash against me,

I still think of you.

When I'm driving down the road

And a song all too familiar plays,

I still think of you.

When I'm laying in bed

And I get a random text,

I still think of you.

Love must be forgotten,

But its hard when you are everywhere.

How you were able

to move on so fast

Is really beyond me.

While you entertain

However many guys

I cant deal with even one.

Instead I'm stuck with

The heartbreak and betrayal

Which ceases to leave me alone.

We hear the phrase "right person wrong timing,"

But I've come to the conclusion thats not true.

How could they be the person right for you

When they can give you up so easily?

How could timing then even matter?

Timing is never perfect,

Neither are the circumstances.

Yet I believe that the right person will find the

effort and hold on to what they dont want to lose.

These days I look within

Reminding myself of whats there.

The love that I crave

Its already sitting in one place.

Theres no future left for me and you

And although I wish that weren't true

My heart and mind wont even argue.

Vacant love and empty promises

Are not something I want to renew.

If you think I cant hold my own

That sooner or later ill be back

Perhaps fall apart without you

Believe me when I say you're a fool.

POF

Letting go is hard

Knowing what you've created

Him being one of the good ones

These days they're hard to come by.

Misery lingers in the uncertainty

That you will find another

Our options are so slim that

"Plenty of Fish" seems unlikely.

What is there to look back on?

But a chapter thats already finished.

Why go back and read it?

When you already know the ending.

That story was already written

And so it was told

Continue moving forward

Let your life's journey unfold.

Starting Over

Late Nights

Empty Bed

Dry Phone

Zero Men

Feeling Lonely

Eerie Silence

No Attention

Times Slower

Little Patience

Heavy Thoughts

You thought you had healed

Moved on, and forgot about him

Even the weight of the hurt seemed minimal.

Until eventually it caught up to you

Its force being heavy and inescapable.

Sometimes all that you can do

Is just lay in bed with the pain

Crying it out, and hoping for better days.

The thought of you

Once kept me in awe.

Now I cant help but

Feel genuine disgust.

Had I known then what I know now

Things would've been much different.

Yet though my fight for love brought

Moments of torment and suffering

Lessons came into full bloom.

Life exhibits duality, with the good

Must also come the bad.

Even though I was surrounded

By a tremendous bag of hurt

Growth was also beginning to arise.

I put back the pieces

That you tore apart

Slowly but surely I am rebuilding.

Its taken a lot of strength

Commitment too,

But I'm finally happy with where Im at.

Honestly, I hope the same for you.

<u>Dont open it (and if you do, slam it shut)</u>

One day he will realize what he did

That he was wrong all along.

He will try to make his way back

Knocking at your hearts door

And you will have to make a choice

Whether to let him in, or to ignore it.

I hope that you come to your senses

And have the courage to shut him out

You deserve somebody who would've stayed.

I still hold space for you in my heart

But that doesn't mean I want a restart.

Honestly, I never thought id get this far

It was like it was yesterday

When life felt so rough.

Your absence was damaging

My spirit felt lifeless

Any hope that I had was gone.

Now I breath in optimism

And my mind is less of a clutter.

Although your absence still hits home

I no longer feel alone.

Gratitude

You broke me down

Took away my self confidence

Stripped me of my joy

Silenced my laughter

Repressed all my motivation.

Yet in the end I discovered

Talents, passions, and desires

That I didn't even know existed.

Your decision to end things

Freed my soul from its chamber

After being dormant for so long.

Who knew that you leaving

Would lead me to finding

My own strengths and possibilities.

Your chosen absence is the greatest

Gift you could've ever given me.

For that, I express gratitude.

What Lies Ahead

It has taken me a long time

Many days and many hours

To feel like I am whole again.

The sourness has gone

Old me has left.

My foundation was shaken

And in the midst

I embraced the need for adaptation.

Through change and growth

I have become even greater.

Cheers to new beginnings.

Damage doesn't go away overnight

Ive learned to give it time

To give myself some space

Grieve and relax

Become free from all the stress.

I allow myself to feel

Because I truly do want to heal

Everyday is a new day

Another moment for transformation.

The process is a journey

Never linear nor complete

I look back and laugh

As I sit with who I've become

Life is truly bittersweet.

Someday you'll look back

And be glad that they left.

What started out as a scandal

Leaving your heart in a million pieces

Only to show you that you could handle.

That ending had to come into fruition

So that other beginnings could start.

The slow beginning of finding yourself again

In the midst of a broken heart.

You can try hiding or running away

Objecting yourself to consumption

Blocking out and ignoring reality.

The truth of the matter is, that

However you choose to drown the

Uneasiness that lies within your body

Will only continue to give it life

Leaving you in constant disappointment.

Pain wants to be heard

Pain wants to be seen

Pain wants to be felt.

It demands to be acknowledged

Before even considering departure.

I'll probably deal with heartbreak again

Maybe even more than once.

However, what I do know

Is that I am now prepared.

The lessons from the past

Have taught and shown me

What is to come

What is to be expected.

No matter how much it hurts

Please put yourself first.

It is better to hurt now

Then to hurt later.

I promise you, that in the end

He will put himself first

Even at the expense

Of leaving you

To fend for yourself.

<u>I am not who I was yesterday</u>

I could've stayed a victim.

I could've placed blame.

I could've remained the same person.

Instead, I took the cards I was dealt

And turned them into tools of growth.

"Everything happens for a reason"

Is exactly what I felt.

I have forgiven myself

For what I did not know.

I have credited myself

For the fact that I still stand.

I am not who I was yesterday

He no longer exists.

Growth really does change you.

I tend to ask myself a lot

Why is it so hard?

I think we can all agree

Life can be a bitch

That includes love too.

Pain is not weakness

On the bad days

Focus on the present.

Sit outside and listen to the birds

Feel the warmth of the sun on your face.

Pay attention and listen to the wind

Rustling the leaves in all the trees.

Those feelings of hurt and despair

Sit through and feel them.

Remember that nothing lasts forever

For everything shall pass.

Ive learned that I love hard. Some may even say that I have high expectations. However it wasn't always that way. Trials and tribulations in the face of love have brought me to this point of certainty. Firmness in the belief that I will not water myself down at the expense of someone else dangling their bare minimum in front of me and calling it love. No thanks.

I used to spend my time

Chasing what I thought was love.

The bare minimum stood out

Not realizing it was just a lack of effort.

I kept chasing and chasing

Wondering why I couldn't receive it.

Turns out there was nothing to find.

That love already existed

Deep within myself and sitting all alone

Waiting for me to come home and find it.

Lesson #???

Dont question the shade of the flag

If its Red then its Red.

Dont try and convince yourself

That you can make it Green.

You are not a magician.

Love is going to show up

When you least expect it.

What you always wanted

Deserve to be exact

Will find its way to you.

As you glance towards him

You'll reflect on the times

Where you would wonder if

Love would ever find you again.

His eyes will meet yours

And in that fraction of intimacy

A spark of realization will ignite,

That he is who you have longed for.

Im just another hopeless romantic trying not to get caught up in the deceit that "love" seems to offer. Staying clear from the chasing, which can be way too time consuming and harmful in the long run. Im no longer interested in denying myself the emotional nourishment that I know I deserve. Let me wait for the right person. After all, isn't love just a waiting game?

Self Compassion

Blindly we are persuaded by temptation

As love leads us into a world unknown.

Many of us end up falling off its tracks

So forgive yourself if you were ignorant.

Seasons

Love comes and goes

Just like the seasons.

Sometimes its temporary

Not always having a reason.

Though death is written in scripture

Remember that rebirth also plays

A part of the bigger picture.

New love always awaits.

Still trying to find my place in this world

I know that I deserve to take up space too.

(We all do. Yes even YOU.)

Self love is a constant journey

Where sometimes, ill admit

I still have trouble loving myself.

Learning how to love myself

Is so much more difficult

On the bad days and through

The times of discomfort.

Self sabotage tends to fill

The empty spaces of my mind

Just waiting for me to give up

Or revert back to my old habits.

In those moments, I desperately

Find the temptation easier than

The discipline needed to continue

Moving forward, not looking back.

Im not perfect, and slip ups are common

But my drive towards loving myself

Is far greater than the weight of

Harming myself like in the past.

Im trying and giving it my best.

I thank myself for showing up for me.

As I close out my voice on paper, I hope that whoever is reading this, realizes just how much we all share. In the adversary that we face against ourselves, while looking for opportunities of love, sometimes the opportunity is within. We seek to create connection amongst what can be a rocky terrain. However, no matter how rough it can get, know that you are not alone. We all face turmoil, whether its external or internal. Our stories may be different, but we share the same desires. Everybody longs to be loved. Its one of the ordinaries that make us human. Though being gay makes it different, or even feel that much harder, never give up hope. In your quest for discovering what you deserve, I hope my experiences can show you, that somewhere else, somebody just like you, does understand. With that, I hope you find peace of mind.

Made in United States
Troutdale, OR
10/10/2023

13577453R00076